My Special
Bedtime Bear

Claire Freedman • Daniel Howarth

GULLANE
CHILDREN'S BOOKS

The sun smiled a sleepy goodbye.
Fireflies flitted through the shadowy woods.
"Time for a special little bear to be
tucked up in bed," called Mummy Bear.
"Am I a special little bear?" Little Bear asked, bouncing over.
"Very special," Mummy Bear smiled.

Mummy Bear took Little Bear's paw.
Together they headed home
through the tall swaying trees.

At Fox's Deep Den, Little Fluffy Fox
was having his bath.

"Little Fluffy Fox and his mummy are having lots of splashy fun!" laughed Little Bear. "Just like *my* bath-time!" "Yes," Mummy Bear agreed, "but your bath-time is extra splashy-special to me! Do you know why?"

Little Bear thought hard, but he couldn't work out why his bath-time was extra-special.

A glowing light shone in Bunny Burrow as they ambled by.
Little Bouncy Bunny was listening as her daddy read her a story.

"They look happy reading together,"
said Little Bear. "Just like *our* story time."
"Yes, they do!" Mummy Bear said. "But your story
time is even more happy-special to me!"

Little Bear tried to think why . . .

In Hedgehog's Hollow, Little Huggy Hedgehog
was being tucked up in bed by his mummy.

"They look cosy!" Little Bear sighed.
"Just like when you put *me* to bed, Mummy."
"Yes!" agreed Mummy Bear. "But tucking you into bed is extra
cosy-special to me! You must have guessed why by now?"

Little Bear shook his head.

Soft breezes rustled the
leaves as Mummy Bear carried
Little Bear gently across
the starlit stream.

Half hidden in the wavy grass was Vole's Hole. Little Roly
Vole was wrapped in a cosy blanket, having his goodnight cuddle.
"That's snuggly!" cried Little Bear. "Just like my goodnight cuddles."
"Your goodnight cuddles are much more snuggly-special to me,"
smiled Mummy Bear. "Surely you know why?"

"No, I don't," said Little Bear.

Bright moonbeams silvered the path
as Little Bear and Mummy Bear
reached Bear Cave.

Mummy Bear gave Little Bear his
splashy bath in front of the fire . . .

then they happily read a story together.

"Hop into bed," said Mummy Bear
as she tucked him in all warm and cosy.
"Mummy," yawned Little Bear sleepily,
"my bedtime *is* extra-special . . . but you still
haven't told me *why*!"

Mummy Bear smiled.
"Because it's spent with . . .

YOU, *Little Bear!*
You are the extra-special part!"

"I *am* a special little bear!" smiled Little Bear
as his heavy eyes began to close.

But then he'd known that all along!